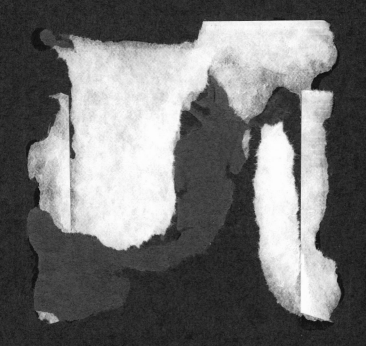

MOLLIE HUNTER

Day of the Unicorn

A Knight of the
Golden Plain Story

ILLUSTRATED BY
DONNA DIAMOND

HarperCollins*Publishers*

Library of Congress Cataloging-in-Publication Data

Hunter, Mollie, date

Day of the unicorn / by Mollie Hunter ; illustrated by Donna Diamond.

p.   cm. — (A Knight of the Golden Plain story)

Summary: A young boy's daydream transforms him into the fearless Sir Dauntless and he sets out to capture a unicorn that has magically escaped from a tapestry at Crag Castle.

ISBN 0-06-021062-1. — ISBN 0-06-021063-X (lib. bdg.)

[1. Knights and knighthood—Fiction.   2. Unicorns—Fiction.   3. Magic— Fiction.]   I. Donna Diamond, Ill.   II. Title.   III. Series: Hunter, Mollie, date Knight of the Golden Plain story.

PZ7.H9176Day   1994   91-44763

[Fic]—dc20   CIP

                                                                              AC

1   2   3   4   5   6   7   8   9   10

❖

First Edition

For JOY,
our joy.

MH

If you had all the daydream adventures
in the world to choose from, which
would be your favorite?
There was a boy once who chose to
daydream about being the fearless and noble
Knight of the Golden Plain. And in one of
the adventures he had then . . .

CHAPTER

1

The Knight of the Golden Plain had been given a message—an urgent one. There was a maiden in distress, and she was pleading with him to come to her aid!

It was a Saturday when this happened, and he was all ready to ride forth in search of some great adventure—Saturday, of course, being the best of all days for this.

His trusty sword of many battles was belted around the scarlet jerkin that went over his armor of silvery chain mail. His white cloak with its shining embroidery of silver thread was slung over one shoulder. He had the scarlet reins of his big, black horse, Midnight, gathered in his hands.

But, as all good knights should do, he decided instantly to ride instead to the aid of this unhappy maiden. Besides which, the message had come from Lady Dorabella of Crag Castle—beautiful Dorabella of the sapphire-blue eyes and hair of moonlit gold! And she was the girl he meant to marry—someday, that is, after he had ridden forth on many other adventures.

"Follow me!" commanded the knight,

Sir Dauntless, urging Midnight into a gallop and beckoning the messenger on with him.

But Dorabella's message had been carried by her page, a small, red-haired boy called Benison, and Benison was mounted only on a fat little pony. The swift and powerful stride of Midnight soon outdistanced this, and Sir Dauntless thundered on alone to Crag Castle.

Faster and faster yet he rode, till the thudding noise of Midnight's hooves began to echo off what seemed like a great dark rock looming up before him. But to the keen eyes of Sir Dauntless, this was more than a rock.

It was Crag Castle itself, and the moment its towers and battlements came into his view, a sentry sounded the trumpet that announced the approach of a mounted knight. Dogs barked. Horses stamped in their stalls. Cooks scolded kitchen maids running to join pages and chambermaids peering for a view of the knight. Stableboys rushed eagerly into the courtyard.

"Whoa, Midnight!" Sir Dauntless pulled the great charger to a skidding halt among the excited stableboys. In one movement, then, he was out of the saddle and tossing the reins to them.

The great doors of the castle gaped wide, and he went through them at a run, his sword held ready for action. The sound of voices raised in anger drew him instantly to the castle's great hall. Boldly he strode into the hall.

Dorabella was there—as yet unharmed, he was relieved to see. Her mother, the Lady Honoria, and her father, Sir Veritas, were there too. So also was the brother of Sir Veritas, a huge and awkward-looking knight called Sir Maladroit. And there

6

was no doubt that they were all in trouble of some kind.

Lady Honoria was using a large lace handkerchief to mop tears from her kindly face. The noble features of Sir Veritas wore a look of great annoyance. The big knight, Sir Maladroit, was shambling about in a very agitated manner; and as soon as Dorabella saw Sir Dauntless, she rushed towards him, crying:

"Oh, save us, Sir Dauntless! Save us, I beg of you!"

"Dry your tears, lady," Sir Dauntless soothed her—because indeed there *were* tears glittering in Dorabella's great sapphire-blue eyes. "You will come to no harm now that I am here to protect you. But save you from what—from whom? That is the first thing I must know."

"From him!" cried Dorabella, pointing

dramatically to the big knight. "From my uncle, Sir Maladroit, and the terrible danger he is now to us all!"

Sir Dauntless could not see anything especially terrible about Sir Maladroit. He was very big, certainly, but he also seemed to be in great pain, because he had a hand clapped to one side of his face and was groaning loudly. But even so, that did not make Sir Dauntless any the less gallant towards Dorabella.

Gently he put her aside, and then, with the light of battle in his eyes, he turned to Sir Maladroit.

"Sir," he said sternly, "you will answer to me for the distress you have caused my lady. And be assured that I am always instantly ready to use my sword in her defense!"

CHAPTER

2

Dorabella went pink with pride at these brave words from Sir Dauntless. But Lady Honoria squeaked with alarm at the sound of them, Sir Maladroit only groaned all the louder, and Sir Veritas cried:

"No, no, Sir Dauntless! There is no

need for swordplay. My brother is not wicked. He is simply foolish, and that is where the danger to us now lies."

Sir Dauntless cast a puzzled look at Sir Maladroit. "Explain yourself, sir," he demanded. "What danger is this?"

"Oh, for goodness' sake!" groaned Sir Maladroit. "All that's happened here is that I have this terrible toothache! And they've been trying to stop me from curing it with a magic charm I got from a Gypsy woman—because they're afraid, you see. They're afraid that the magic might bring disaster on them at the same time as it brings a cure for me."

"And it will do that! It will!" cried Lady Honoria. "Because you have an absolute talent for creating disaster, haven't you?"

"Indeed he has," snapped Sir Veritas, "right from the time we were little boys

11

together and any toy he offered to mend always ended up in a worse state than it was in before."

"And that's just what will happen here," cried Dorabella, "if we are foolish enough now to trust *him* with working magic!"

"You are right, my lady," Sir Dauntless agreed, quite convinced now that it would indeed be foolish to let this clumsy knight meddle with anything so dangerous as magic. But try as he would then, he could not persuade Sir Maladroit to listen to a single word of his arguments against using the charm.

"Because," Sir Maladroit declared, "I have already listened to more than enough on that score. Besides which, it's such a simple piece of magic really—but look, I'll show you."

With one hand outstretched to show

Sir Dauntless a small, open box that held some white powder, Sir Maladroit moved towards the fire blazing brightly in the fireplace of the great hall.

"Now," he said, "there are only two things I have to do to remove my toothache and make it settle elsewhere. I have to recite the words of the charm; but first—I have to throw this powder onto the fire!"

Before anyone could make the slightest move to stop him then, Sir Maladroit tossed the powder onto the fire. Immediately, the flames there sank down to the merest flicker; and in instant fear of what might come next, Sir Veritas shouted:

"The words, Sir Dauntless, the words of the charm! Don't let him say them."

Sir Dauntless was leaping forward even as Sir Veritas shouted, his sword pointing straight at Sir Maladroit. But the big knight had expected this. Sword in hand, he swung round to meet the leap.

Their weapons clashed. The hall began to ring with the sound of steel on steel. But big as Sir Maladroit was, it was soon clear to him and everyone else that he was no match for a swordsman as skillful as the Knight of the Golden Plain!

Step by step he had to back from the flashing blade of Sir Dauntless. His defense grew more and more awkward. His sword began to waver in his hand—until at last came the masterstroke that sent it spinning right out of his grasp.

With his back to the wall, then, and the quivering blade of Sir Dauntless pointed straight at his heart, he cried out desperately:

"I still do not yield, Sir Dauntless. I do not yield!"

"But you must," Sir Dauntless told

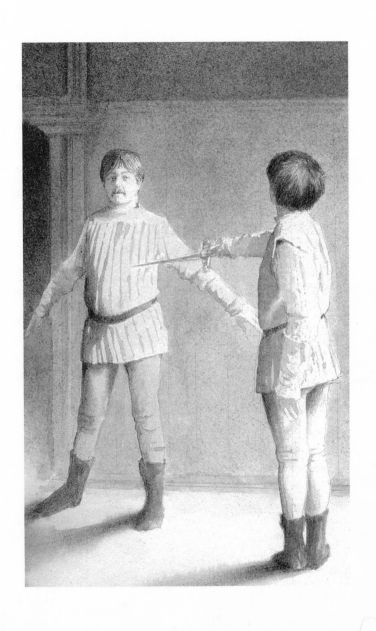

him. "I have disarmed you."

"Then kill me!" Sir Maladroit retorted. "Because that is the *only* way now to stop me from reciting the words of the magic charm!"

Sir Dauntless drew back in horror at this. "Sir Maladroit," he protested, "I cannot stain my knightly honor by killing an unarmed man."

"Then you must all take the consequences," Sir Maladroit told him, "because I cannot any longer suffer the pain of this toothache."

And, while they all stood helpless before this declaration, he began chanting:

"Out of the gum,
And out of the tooth,
Into the horn,
And into the hoof,
I conjure now the pain, the pain,

I conjure now the pain.
Out of the flesh,
And out of the bone,
Into the beast
That lives alone,
And there shall it remain, remain.
And there shall it remain. "

The harsh voice of Sir Maladroit rang out like the sound of iron striking stone. And the moment he had uttered the last word of the charm, the fire that had been almost dead shot up in a lightning sheet of flame.

But it was only the wall above the fireplace that was lit by this sheet of flame. And all that anyone could see then was the figure at the center of the tapestry that hung there—the huge white figure of a unicorn, rearing within a circle of leafy branches, with the single horn on

17

its forehead pointing towards the upper arch of this encircling greenery.

The brilliant flash of light vanished as suddenly as it had come. And just as suddenly then, the great hall was filled with a black and utter darkness.

Along with the darkness came a smell—a strong animal smell. There was a thundering noise also, like the sound of great hooves galloping, and a rush of wind that was like the passing of something fast and heavy.

Lady Honoria screamed. Sir Veritas and Sir Maladroit shouted their alarm; and it was only Sir Dauntless, in the midst of all this, who kept his head.

With outstretched hands he groped around to find Dorabella so that he could protect her from whatever should happen next; and was just in time to catch her as she fainted clean away, into his arms.

CHAPTER

3

The sound of hooves vanished. So did the strong animal smell; and with their disappearance, the terrible darkness lifted also from the hall. Dorabella came back to her senses; and then, just as everybody else was doing, she stared at the tapestry above the fireplace.

There was a great, gaping hole in it now, where once the figure of the unicorn had been! The circle of leafy branches that had once surrounded the figure was now only a circle of broken green threads, and the whole of the tapestry itself hung loose from the wall.

Dorabella felt like fainting again when she saw all this. But Sir Dauntless would not have been near enough at that moment to catch her. Besides which, it was just then that her page, Benison, came running into the hall, shouting in great excitement as he ran:

"A marvel has happened—a marvel! I have just seen a unicorn! I was making my way back here when a *unicorn* went rushing past me!"

"Oh, do be quiet, Benison!" snapped Lady Honoria. "It would have been a much greater marvel if you had *not* seen

that unicorn—considering that it has only just broken loose from the tapestry up there."

Benison gaped up at the torn tapestry, his small, round face a picture of bewilderment. "But—but how?" he stammered. "How *could* such a thing happen?"

"Quite simply," Dorabella told him. "Sir Maladroit managed to use his magic spell in spite of everything Sir Dauntless could do to stop him. The spell took the toothache away from him, and cast it instead on 'the beast that lives alone'— which, of course, is the unicorn, because every unicorn always does live alone—"

"And of course also," Lady Honoria interrupted bitterly, "the spell fell on *our* unicorn, because it was the one nearest to him. And that was what enraged it enough to make it break loose from the tapestry."

"But excuse me, my lady," Benison objected. "That only tells me *why* the unicorn broke loose. You still haven't told me *how*."

"Benison," Sir Veritas said gravely, "you are asking us to explain magic. But it would take wiser heads than ours to do that."

"And do not forget, Benison," Dorabella added, "that the unicorn itself is a magical animal."

"Are you listening to us?" demanded Lady Honoria, rounding on Sir Maladroit. "Why didn't *you* take account of all these things before you spoke the words of your spell?"

"I forgot," mumbled Sir Maladroit. "The toothache was so bad, you see, it just made me forget everything I'd ever learned about unicorns."

He turned away from her, looking so

ashamed of himself that they all felt
suddenly sorry for him. But sympathy for
this awkward knight still did not make
any difference to the fact that there would
be no peace or safety for anyone so long as
a creature as wild and dangerous as the
unicorn was on the loose. And it was Sir
Dauntless, then, who took charge of the
situation.

"Give me a rope," he said briskly, "and
I will recapture the unicorn." Benison
ran off immediately to fetch a rope, but
Dorabella cried:

"No, no, Sir Dauntless! That would be
too dangerous!"

"Of course it would," agreed the Lady
Honoria, "because it's not as if this is just
any unicorn. This one, don't forget, has a
toothache!"

"We're all aware of that, my dear," Sir
Veritas told her. "But it will still be much

more dangerous—not only for us, but for everyone—if Sir Dauntless does *not* recapture it."

"And I will go with him to do that!" Sir Maladroit volunteered. "I don't have a toothache now, after all. And I'm *very* strong."

It was a generous offer, thought Sir Dauntless. But, on the other hand, the very last person he wanted to have with him in moments of peril was a bungler like Sir Maladroit!

"I thank you, sir," he answered courteously. "And I am sure you are as brave as you are strong. But I still prefer to follow my custom of riding alone—except sometimes for a page to perform certain duties for me. And on this occasion, I will take the page Benison to guide me in the direction he saw the unicorn heading."

"I'll do that gladly, sir!" exclaimed

Benison, coming back at that moment with a great coil of rope over his shoulder.

"Then let us waste no more time," ordered Sir Dauntless. He bowed to Lady Honoria, and gave a salute of farewell to Sir Veritas and Sir Maladroit. Gallantly, then, he knelt to kiss Dorabella's hand.

"I will repair the harm done by Sir Maladroit," he promised. And with Benison proudly following, he strode forth to recapture the unicorn.

CHAPTER

4

Side by side Sir Dauntless and Benison rode out from the castle, with Sir Dauntless carrying the coil of rope slung over his saddlebow.

Benison, on his fat little pony, looked smaller than ever beside Sir Dauntless mounted high on his great black charger.

But, small as Benison was, he still had the ambition that one day he too would be a knight. And to help him learn about knighthood, he was eager to remain as long as possible, that day, at the side of Sir Dauntless.

"That way, sir!" he cried, pointing to some distant trees. "It went that way—towards the Great Green Deep."

"You have sharp eyes, lad," approved Sir Dauntless, trying not to look dismayed at the thought of entering a place as mysterious as the Great Green Deep. "That could well be useful to me—and so forward, now, Benison! Forward!"

Benison whooped with delight at this command, and urged his pony to a gallop that just managed to keep up with the swift, cantering pace of Midnight.

A gap opened out among the distant trees—a gap that proved to be the en-

trance to a wide, tree-lined ravine, or
canyon; and soon they were riding down
into this canyon.

Down, down, and down into it they
rode, with the trees that lined its sides
now growing ever taller and thinner as
they stretched upwards to reach the light.

Still farther down they went till they
were deep, deep below the ordinary sur-
face of the earth; and there, on level
ground at last, they found themselves at
the very heart of the Great Green Deep.

"Keep a good lookout for the unicorn,"
Sir Dauntless told Benison then. But he
gave his order in a voice that was little
more than a whisper, for this was a place
even more mysterious than he had
thought it would be—a place that seemed
somehow to be waiting for something to
happen in it!

All around were slender trees so tall

that the two of them were quite dwarfed by this soaring height. The undergrowth between the tall trees stretched away in a haze, a fuzz, an endless mist of green. And high overhead was a canopy of leaves so thick that even the daylight filtering through it had a greenish tinge.

Underfoot, also, there was a thick carpet of green moss, and this so completely muffled all sound of hoofbeats that their mounts could have been ghost horses padding over it.

Benison shivered as this same thought occurred to him also, and nervously he asked: "We'll not hear it, sir, will we, if it comes charging towards us?"

"Yes, we will," Sir Dauntless told him. "We'll hear bushes breaking, branches being snapped, and—"

The very sounds he was describing broke suddenly on their hearing. At the same time, there was a waft of the strong animal smell that had occurred in the great hall of Crag Castle. A sound rang out, a sound that was halfway between a roar and a scream.

"Take cover, Benison!" Sir Dauntless shouted, lifting the coil of rope from his saddlebow. "The unicorn—it's coming this way!"

Benison wheeled his pony around. Sir Dauntless drew rein, keeping his gaze steady on the direction of the sounds that warned of the unicorn's approach. And seconds later, in that direction, he saw branches being hurled into the air, small trees bending, bushes that swayed.

There was a flash of something white, then a larger gleam of white. The animal smell grew overpoweringly strong. Midnight reared up in alarm. Midnight's nostrils had caught that smell even more keenly than his own had, Sir Dauntless realized, and it was making the great horse terribly uneasy.

"Steady," he soothed. "Steady now." But brave as Midnight undoubtedly was, it was still asking too much of a creature of flesh and blood to stand steady in face of the approach of a fabulous monster!

Midnight would not be soothed; and so, Sir Dauntless decided, there was only one way out of this dilemma—the bold way. He would have to inspire Midnight to a charge that would meet the onward rush of the unicorn.

Swiftly, on this decision, he tightened his grip on the reins, dug his heels sharply into Midnight's sides, and yelled his battle cry:

"A Dauntless! A Dauntless!"

Like a trumpet calling the signal to attack, the sound of that cry rang out across the Great Green Deep; and immediately, as it had always done before, the battle-hardened Midnight responded by launching itself into a great, forward bound.

Horse and rider went crashing through the mass of greenery ahead; but over the noise of their charging advance came again that half scream, half roar they had already heard from the unicorn. And it was nearer now, much nearer—a truly dreadful sound that was like all the rage in the world suddenly finding a voice!

Midnight's stride faltered. Sir Dauntless tried not to think of the long, sharp horn jutting from the unicorn's forehead.

The raging voice came closer yet—so close that its sound echoed all around them. There was nothing now between them and the unicorn except a light screen of greenery. Sir Dauntless balanced his rope for the throw that would land a noose around the creature's neck.

The greenery ahead exploded into a whirlwind of leaves and branches. And

out of the heart of the whirlwind charged the unicorn, its great white body hurtling like a thunderbolt towards them. Midnight swerved from the wicked point of its jutting horn, and the move unbalanced Sir Dauntless.

The thunderbolt struck—and Sir Dauntless knew no more.

CHAPTER

Sir Dauntless was quite some time in coming back to his senses, and the first thing he saw then was Benison's pony. But there was no sign of Midnight, nor was Benison himself there. Yet still he was not alone!

There was a woman standing in front

of him. She was dressed in a long, flowing gown of green, with a light veil of the same color over her head and swathed around her neck. But dress and veil were so exactly the green of the bushes on either side of her that it was really only her face which allowed Sir Dauntless to tell her apart from them.

He sat up, staring at her, and asked in wonder:

"Who are you, lady? Where did *you* come from?"

"I have always been here," she told him. "Where there are green and growing things, that is where you will always find me. I am the Dame of the Great Green Deep."

She had a very dignified manner, thought Sir Dauntless. Also, she was not young, and so she was well suited to the title of "Dame." She smiled at him, a

sympathetic smile that made him wonder suddenly how badly hurt he was.

Carefully he rose, and discovered to his great relief that he was not hurt at all. That last-second swerve by Midnight, he realized, had meant that the charge of the unicorn had hit them both side on. Also, the soft moss had cushioned his fall. And so now, if he could only find Midnight again . . .

Hastily, he said, "I am pleased to have made your acquaintance, Dame. But I beg you to excuse me now while I search for my horse, Midnight; also for a page boy, Benison, who came here with me on a task of knightly honor."

"You will not find either of them here," answered the Dame of the Great Green Deep; "because, when Benison came looking for you, I sent him off on Midnight, to tell the Lady Dorabella of what has happened—and also of what will happen if you do not listen to me now."

"In that case, Dame," said Sir Dauntless, dismayed by the way she seemed to have meddled in his plans, "I fear you have taken a great liberty. Also, since I must now go on foot, you have made it a thousand times harder for me to recapture the unicorn, and thus to fulfill the promise I have made to my lady."

"But you never will be able to do so," the Dame told him, "because—"

"Do you doubt my courage for the task?" Sir Dauntless interrupted, staring in amazement at her. And quickly the Dame assured him:

"No, no! Not for a moment. But the unicorn, remember, is a magical animal. Also, there are rules to magic, as there are to everything—which means that you have no choice now but to accept the rule of magic, which says that the unicorn can yield to no one except a young maiden."

"But Dame!" exclaimed Sir Dauntless, staring in horror at such an idea. "What young maiden would face so dreadful a creature as the unicorn?"

Quietly the Dame said, "Dorabella would. Dorabella truly loves you, Sir Dauntless. And that is why—for your sake—she would face the unicorn."

"No!" shouted Sir Dauntless. "No! I cannot allow such a thing to happen!"

"In other words," said the Dame, her voice now cold and hard, "you are no true knight. Because, Sir Dauntless, you do not have the highest of all kinds of courage—the kind that will force you to stand by and let your lady prove herself to be as brave as the lady of every knight should be."

In his heart of hearts, then, Sir

Dauntless realized that the Dame of the Great Green Deep had spoken a great truth. If Dorabella really *was* brave enough to face the unicorn, he would indeed be no true knight if he could not show the kind of courage that would allow her to prove this to be so. Yet still he could not bear the thought of her in such danger, and in desperation he cried:

"But this is not just *any* unicorn! This one has a toothache!"

"It *had* a toothache," the Dame corrected. "But that is no longer so, either for the unicorn itself *or* the foolish Sir Maladroit—because here, in the Great Green Deep, are the magical healing herbs needed to banish the pain of that forever. I have made it my task to guide the unicorn to them—and that also was part of my message to Dorabella."

"But even so," Sir Dauntless persisted,

"the unicorn is still a wild and dangerous creature. And I still cannot bear to let her face it for love of me unless she knows I truly love her in return. Yet how can she know that when I have never told her so?"

"Do as I say now," the Dame instructed, "and she will know. Sit down, close your eyes, and think only of Dorabella."

Sir Dauntless hesitated, but only for a moment. There was no other way now, after all, of letting Dorabella know that he truly loved her. And so he had to do as the Dame had said. Slowly he sat down, closed his eyes, and thought of Dorabella.

A picture of Dorabella came into his mind—Dorabella's gentle face, Dorabella's hair of moonlit gold and eyes of starry sapphire blue. His whole heart filled with love of Dorabella, and just as he was thinking that this was the most

wonderful feeling in the world, the Dame told him:

"Now open your eyes." And once again, Sir Dauntless did as she had said.

There was a bird fluttering in front of him—a small bird with feathers of brilliant blue. The bird circled once around his head; and then, like a bright-blue jewel flung suddenly upward, it soared into full flight, rising swiftly higher and higher until it disappeared through the canopy of leaves above the Great Green Deep.

Sir Dauntless watched every moment of its flight. And as he did so, he had the strangest feeling that this bright little creature was the very embodiment of his love for Dorabella, and that it would fly straight towards her. The moment he thought so, too, the Dame of the Great Green Deep cried:

"That is the bird called Halcyon—the messenger that can be sent only from a heart that truly loves to another heart that loves as truly!"

With joy, then, Sir Dauntless turned to thank her for showing him this way of telling Dorabella that he did truly love her. But in the place where the Dame had stood there was now only a green bush that looked no different from any of the bushes beside it.

CHAPTER

6

*S*ir Dauntless did not really have long to wait for Dorabella's arrival in the Great Green Deep. Yet still the time seemed dreadfully long to him before he saw her at last, mounted on her own white pony, Snowfire, with Benison following, perched high on Midnight.

The little blue bird was circling around her head as she rode, glittering bright against the soft gold of her long hair. Sir Dauntless rushed to help her dismount; and it was not until he did so that the bird soared once more into full flight. Joyfully then, as it sped upwards towards the canopy of leaves, he exclaimed:

"So it *did* fly straight from me to you!"

"And I did not need to be told it was the bird of love," Dorabella responded eagerly. "*Or* that it was you who had sent it to me. I knew all that in my heart, the moment I saw it—and so I am all the more inspired now, to face the unicorn!"

She was very pale, all the same, Sir Dauntless noticed; and much distressed by this, he cried:

"But I am afraid to let you face it, Dorabella! I am terribly afraid."

"You must not be," she told him. "You

must think only that I do so gladly, for love of you."

Without letting him say another word, then, she walked to a clear space beside the nearest line of bushes. And there, with her gaze fixed on the greenery ahead and keeping perfectly still, she stood waiting for the unicorn to appear.

"Tie up the horses, Benison," ordered Sir Dauntless, "in case they bolt in panic from the unicorn's approach." Benison hurried to obey; but the long time of waiting after that made him so nervous that he was driven to whisper urgently at last:

"Sir, should you not have your sword ready to protect the Lady Dorabella?"

Sir Dauntless sighed. "No, Benison. I will be no true knight if I cannot have the courage to stand aside to let my lady prove *her* courage. And so this is one occasion where I must *not* draw my sword."

A sudden waft of the unicorn's strong animal smell made the horses snort and try to break free. The bushes in front of Dorabella swayed, and Sir Dauntless fought strongly against the impulse to spring forward to her. The bushes swayed again, and out from among them stepped the unicorn.

It was huge, and white as newly fallen snow. It had the head and body of a horse, the legs of a deer, the tail of a lion. A deep groove wound in a spiral all the way up its long, sharp horn. The horn itself was white at the base, black in the middle, red at the tip; and its eyes, too, were red— fiery red!

It stood perfectly still, confronting Dorabella. She faced it, standing just as still.

The unicorn began to move slowly forward. Sir Dauntless clenched his fists and felt every muscle in his body grow tense. Dorabella did not flinch from its approach.

Step by slow step, the unicorn advanced until it was so close to her that she could have reached out and touched it. The panic of the horses grew ever wilder. Sir Dauntless became so afraid for her that he shook in every limb. But still she did not move.

The unicorn began to lower its head. Inch by inch the great head came down, until the sharp red tip of its horn was pointed straight at Dorabella's heart. Once again, with the most enormous effort of will, Sir Dauntless stopped himself from springing forward to her.

The noise of panic from the horses died into sudden silence. For a long, frozen moment there was no sound, no movement, in the whole of the Great

Green Deep. And then Dorabella raised her right hand.

Slowly, gracefully, she raised it. Gently she placed it on the bowed head of the unicorn. A shudder ran the whole length of its gleaming white body. Its fiery eyes dimmed with sudden tears.

The tears spilled over, running down its face. Then suddenly it reared high into the very pose it had held in the tapestry in Crag Castle, its hind legs stretched, its horn pointed up to the surrounding greenery, its great forelegs striking out high above Dorabella's head.

For a moment only it stayed like this. Then it vanished—instantly and completely vanished!

"Dorabella!" shouted Sir Dauntless, finally getting over his astonishment at this. And rushing to clasp her hands in his, he cried admiringly, "You are the bravest lady in the whole wide world!"

"And you," she answered, weeping and laughing all in the one breath, "are the truest of all true knights!"

"But where has it gone?" cried Benison, looking around in bewilderment. "Where?"

And from somewhere in the green all around them came a voice that both he and Sir Dauntless recognized as the voice of the Dame of the Great Green Deep.

"Back to where it belongs," said the voice. "Back to the tapestry in Crag Castle."

There were great sighs of relief all round at this—and from Dorabella an instant plea that they should all hurry back to Crag Castle to view this new marvel.

"Because," said she, "I have grown up with that tapestry unicorn, after all, and Crag Castle will not *be* Crag Castle to me again until I have seen it back in its place there."

Once they had all mounted and ridden out of the Great Green Deep, however, Sir Dauntless realized how much of that day had fled and that—for him at least—there had to be a change of plan.

"Dorabella," he said, "I have promised my lady mother that I would be home in time for tea. And so I regret very much now that I cannot ride back to Crag Castle with you."

Dorabella sighed. "I regret that too," she told him. "But you will come back to Crag Castle again sometime—will you not?"

"I will indeed," Sir Dauntless assured her. "Sometime soon! And meanwhile—" He turned in the saddle to summon Benison. "Look after my lady, Benison," he instructed. "Look after her well."

"I will, sir," Benison said eagerly. "I will guard her as you would—with my life!"

And so off they set again, all three of them. In one direction went the golden-haired lady who, on that day of the unicorn, had so wonderfully proved her courage. Proudly riding escort to her was the page who would surely one day be a knight.

And in the opposite direction, riding home to tea, went the one and only of his kind, that truest of all true knights, Sir Dauntless—

The Knight of the Golden Plain.

59

About the Author

MOLLIE HUNTER is the author of many popular and acclaimed books for young people. She loves to write about the people of her native Scotland—from the distant history of *The Stronghold*, which won a Carnegie Medal, to recollections of her own young-adult years, reflected in *A Sound of Chariots* and its sequel, *Hold On to Love*. Her most recent novel, *The Mermaid Summer*, makes no mention of time or place but is steeped in the magic of the Scottish folklore tradition that Hunter knows so well.

Born in East Lothian of a Scots mother and an Irish father, Mollie Hunter has said she never wanted to be anything but a writer. Her wish came true; as one distinguished American critic proclaimed, she is "Scotland's most gifted storyteller."

Mollie Hunter now lives in a Highland glen near Inverness with her husband, Michael. There she writes, gardens, and tells marvelous stories to her grandchildren.

About the Illustrator

DONNA DIAMOND has illustrated, among many other books, Katherine Paterson's *Bridge to Terabithia*, Shirley Rousseau Murphy's *Song of the Christmas Mouse*, and *Riches* by Esther Hautzig. She lives in Riverdale, NY.